Tess
the Sea Turtle
Fairy

To Rosemary Scarborough, a very special
friend of the fairies!

Special thanks
to Narinder Dhami

ISBN 978-0-545-27039-7

All rights reserved. Published by Scholastic Inc., 557 Broadway, New
York, NY 10012, by arrangement with Rainbow Magic Limited.

12 11 10 9 8 7 6 5 4 3   11 12 13 14 15 16/0

Printed in the U.S.A.   40

This edition first printing, March 2011

Tess

the Sea Turtle Fairy

by Daisy Meadows

LITTLE APPLE

SCHOLASTIC INC.

New York   Toronto   London   Auckland

Sydney   Mexico City   New Delhi   Hong Kong

With the magic conch shell at my side,
I'll rule the oceans far and wide!
But my foolish goblins have shattered the shell,
So now I cast my icy spell.

Seven shell fragments, be gone, I say,
To the human world to hide away,
Now the shell is gone, it's plain to see,
The oceans will never have harmony!

Contents

A Magic Sandcastle

"Should we build another tower, Kirsty?" Rachel Walker asked her best friend, Kirsty Tate.

The two girls were kneeling on the beach making an enormous sandcastle. They'd been working on it all day in the sunshine. The castle had turrets and towers and archways.

"Oh, yes, what a great idea!" Kirsty said with a grin. She picked up her bucket. "Let's start decorating the castle, too. We can use those pretty pink and white shells we found earlier."

Carefully, Rachel began to build the tower. Kirsty poured the shells out of her bucket and began sorting through all of them. "Look, Kirsty, the sun's starting to set," Rachel pointed out, noticing that people were packing up and leaving the beach. "We'll have to go back to your gran's soon." The

girls were spending their spring
vacation in Leamouth with Kirsty's
gran.

Kirsty's face fell. "I know we've had
a good time at the beach, Rachel," she
sighed, "but we
haven't seen
even a *single*
magic fairy
sparkle all
day! I was
hoping we
were going
to find another
missing piece of the magic golden conch
shell."

"Me, too," Rachel agreed. "But don't
forget what Queen Titania always

says—we have to wait
for the magic to
come to us!"

On the first day of
their vacation, the
girls had been thrilled to
receive an invitation to
the Fairyland Ocean Gala. They'd seen
their old friend, Shannon the Ocean
Fairy, there as well as the other Ocean
Fairies and their magic creatures.
The highlight of the gala was to
be the moment when Shannon played
the beautiful golden conch shell. This
would make sure that there was peace,
harmony, and order in all the oceans of
the world for the next year.

But before Shannon had a chance to

play her magic song, Jack Frost and his
goblins had burst into the gala. On Jack
Frost's orders, the goblins had grabbed
the golden conch shell. As they argued
over it, the conch
shell had fallen to
the ground and
smashed into seven
shining pieces!

Jack Frost had
immediately raised his
ice wand and scattered the pieces in
different hiding places throughout the
human world. Shannon, Rachel, Kirsty,
and all the fairies had been horrified.
They knew that without the golden
conch shell, there would be chaos and
confusion in oceans everywhere.

"It doesn't look like any magic is going to come to us today, though," Kirsty remarked. She began pressing rows of tiny, creamy shells onto the sides of the sandcastle. "But at least we've helped the Ocean Fairies find three pieces of the golden conch shell so far."

"And we know that four of the magic ocean creatures are still guarding the four missing pieces," Rachel pointed out.

Luckily, Queen Titania had acted quickly against Jack Frost's spell. The queen had used her own magic to send the Ocean Fairies' magic creatures out into the human world. They would guard the shell pieces until they were safely returned to Fairyland. When all the pieces were back, the golden conch shell could magically repair itself and Shannon would be able to play it at last.

"Isn't our castle great, Rachel?" Kirsty said proudly, sitting back on her heels to take a look. There was hardly anyone left on the beach now except for the two girls.

Rachel nodded. "It looks a bit like the Fairyland Palace with all those towers," she replied. "Except our castle isn't so sparkly, of course!"

Suddenly Kirsty gave an excited cry. "Are you *sure*, Rachel?" she asked with a big smile. "Look in there, under that archway!"

Rachel bent forward on her hands and knees and peered inside the sandcastle. Then she saw it! A glittering, golden light was shining right in the very center of the castle.

"Kirsty, I think it's a fairy!" Rachel gasped as she spotted a tiny figure dancing gracefully through the sandy rooms. "It's Tess the Sea Turtle Fairy!"

Tess fluttered over to the archway and waved up at the girls. She wore cropped blue pants and a pale blue sparkly

T-shirt with an aquamarine sweater over it. Her silky blond hair was parted into two bouncy braids.

"Girls, I'm so glad to see you," Tess called in a silvery voice. "Come and join me inside your beautiful sandcastle!" She pointed her wand at Rachel and Kirsty, and a stream of sparkles swirled around them. The girls felt themselves shrinking like they had so many times before. In the twinkle of an eye, they were fairy-size with beautiful wings just like Tess's.

Quickly, Rachel and Kirsty flew under the archway and joined their fairy friend inside the sandcastle.

"We're really happy to see you, Tess!" Kirsty beamed at the fairy. "Have you found another piece of the golden conch shell?"

Tess nodded. "I think so," she replied. "My magic sea turtle friend, Pearl, is guarding it. But it's in a tropical place far away from here. Will you come with me, girls?"

"Of course we will!" cried Rachel eagerly.

"Gran isn't expecting us home for a little while," Kirsty added. "Let's go right away!"

Turtle Trouble

Waving her wand, Tess flew around
Rachel and Kirsty as they hovered in
the air.

Immediately, a dazzling cloud of fairy
sparkles surrounded the girls. They
closed their eyes and felt themselves
whisked away from Leamouth beach.
They raced through the air at a speed
that took their breath away.

Suddenly the air felt much warmer. Rachel and Kirsty opened their eyes and saw that they were flying over a tropical beach. The ocean was a clear turquoise blue, and the sand was a pure, soft white. Palm trees hugged the shore, their leafy fronds waving in the breeze. Dusk was falling and the pink and gold sun was sinking slowly into the rippling water.

"Isn't it beautiful?" Kirsty sighed happily. She peered down at the beach as it began to get a little darker. "I wish we'd gotten here a bit earlier so that we could see it all in the daytime."

Rachel was squinting down at the beach, too. "What are *those*?" she asked, sounding puzzled. "They look like little polka dots, but they're running around. And there are *lots* of them!"

At first Kirsty couldn't tell what
Rachel meant, but as her eyes adjusted
to the dim light, she could also see little
round shapes. They were scurrying
across the sand in every direction.

"Let's fly closer," said Tess, "and then
you'll be able to see what they are!"

Curious, Rachel and Kirsty followed
Tess as she floated down the beach.

"Oh!" Kirsty exclaimed suddenly. "They're baby sea turtles!"

"They're so cute!" Rachel laughed.

The little green turtles were using their tiny flippers to  move across the beach away from the ocean. As the girls watched, sand flew in all directions and more baby turtles began to appear from holes in the ground.

"Those are the ones that have just hatched," Tess explained. "The mother turtle buries her eggs under the sand."

"But why are all the baby turtles running away from the ocean?" Kirsty asked.

Tess sighed. "When baby sea turtles hatch, they *should* head straight for the water," she explained. "But the poor little things are confused, like the other ocean creatures, because we haven't found all the pieces of the golden conch shell yet!"

Kirsty and Rachel shared an anxious glance. "What will happen to them?" Kirsty asked. "Can we help?"

"Maybe we can carry them to the

ocean and put them in the water,"
Rachel suggested.

"No, there are just too many!" Tess
replied, glancing down at the hundreds
of tiny turtles below them. "We have to
find Pearl. Then she'll be able to lead
the babies safely to the ocean."

"Should we fly
around and
look for
her?" asked
Rachel.

Tess nodded.
"But stay close
to the beach,"
she told them.

Rachel and Tess flew off in different
directions along the beach. Kirsty
drifted over to the palm trees and

began zigzagging slowly between them, looking carefully for Pearl. Suddenly a loud voice erupted from the treetops overhead and made Kirsty jump.

"My feet are cold and wet! I HATE having cold, wet feet!"

Kirsty froze in midair. She glanced up, but couldn't see anything. Quickly she flew back to the beach.

"Rachel! Tess!" Kirsty called to her friends. "Over here!"

"Have you found Pearl?" Rachel asked eagerly as she and Tess rushed to join Kirsty.

"No, but come and listen to this!" Kirsty told them. She led Rachel and Tess over to the palm trees. As they hovered there, they heard a shrill, complaining voice above them.

"My feet are cold and wet, too! There's horrible, itchy sand between my toes!"

Kirsty glanced at Rachel and Tess. "Did you hear that?" she whispered. "Goblins!"

Follow the Leader

Tess frowned. "It definitely *sounds* like goblins," she replied. "We all know they don't like having cold, wet feet! Let's take a look."

Tess flew up toward the voice, and Rachel and Kirsty followed. Suddenly they heard the sound of Tess's tinkling fairy laughter.

"Girls, these are the prettiest goblins I've ever seen!" she called.

Surprised, Rachel and Kirsty flew higher. Then their eyes widened and they also burst out laughing. Four beautiful scarlet-and-blue parrots were perched on the top of the palm tree. As Tess and the girls watched, one of the parrots opened his beak and squawked, "I hate sand!"

"I hate sand!" the parrot sitting beside him repeated fiercely.

"The parrots are mimicking the sound of the goblins grumbling and arguing!" Rachel said with a grin.

"That means there have to be goblins around here *somewhere*," Kirsty pointed out.

Tess nodded. "So it's even more important that we find the missing piece of the golden conch shell before the goblins do," she said anxiously. "I wonder where Pearl is. She's the only one who can help us."

"Let's keep searching," said Rachel.

Tess and the girls flew off along the beach again, above the baby turtles who were still scurrying around. It was almost dark now, but there was a large pale moon. Stars were beginning to sparkle in the midnight-blue sky.

"Doesn't the moonlight make everything look magical?" Kirsty remarked. She stared out over the waves gently lapping on the shore. Then she blinked, wondering if she was seeing things. Was that a gold glow out there on the water, glittering in the light of the moon?

"There's something shiny and sparkly in the ocean!" Kirsty shouted with excitement. "I think it might be a missing piece of the conch shell!"

Rachel and Tess looked over in the direction Kirsty was pointing.

"It looks like the waves are carrying it to the shore," Rachel said, her eyes fixed on the sparkling glow.

"Come on, girls!" Tess cried, heading for the water.

Rachel and Kirsty rushed after her. The three friends stopped and hovered in the air as the glowing object floated closer to the beach.

"It's not a missing piece of the conch shell," Tess exclaimed happily. "It's Pearl!"

Rachel and Kirsty watched the magic green sea turtle swim

gracefully through the waves and onto the shore. Pearl's beautiful shell glittered with fairy magic as she pulled herself higher up on the sand with her strong flippers.

"I'm so glad you found us, Pearl!" Tess flew down and patted the turtle's head. "We need your help."

"The baby turtles are running *away* from the ocean, instead of into it," Rachel explained. "And we know there are goblins around here somewhere, because the parrots are talking just like them!" Kirsty added.

Slowly Pearl nodded her head. Her dark eyes were wise and kind. "Pearl thinks that the missing piece of the shell is around here somewhere, but she's not quite sure where," Tess explained to the girls. "She saw it bobbing around on the waves, but then she lost sight of it. It might have washed up on the shore."

"Maybe we should look after the baby turtles first, and lead them safely to the water," Kirsty suggested. "I'm worried about them! Then we can start searching for the shell."

Rachel glanced down at the beach below them. To her surprise, she saw that the baby turtles had stopped wandering aimlessly away from the ocean. Instead, they were all scuttling along the beach, heading the same way in one big crowd.

"What's going on?" Rachel wondered. Then, at the front of the crowd of turtles, she spotted a group of three kids walking along the beach. One of them was carrying a bucket. "Look," Rachel said in surprise, "I think the baby turtles are following those boys!"

"Let's find out," Tess said. She flew off with Rachel and Kirsty right behind her. Pearl followed them along the sand.

As Tess and the girls got closer to the boys, they noticed something very strange.

"Why are they wearing big straw hats and sunglasses?" Kirsty whispered, frowning. "The sun went down already, and it's dark!"

"Look at their footprints, too." Tess pointed down at the sand. "They have *very* big feet for kids."

"And very big ears!" Rachel said in a low voice, spotting large, pointy ears sticking out of the straw hats. "They're not boys at all. They're goblins!"

Tess, Kirsty, and Rachel shared worried glances.

"Why are the baby turtles following them?" Kirsty asked, confused, glancing down at the large crowd of turtles still scurrying along behind the goblins.

Tess grinned. "Well, the turtles have only just hatched," she replied. "And since they're green, and so are the goblins, the babies think the goblins are grown-up turtles!"

Pogwurzel Panic

Rachel and Kirsty couldn't help but laugh.

"I wonder if the goblins know they're being followed?" said Rachel.

"And *I* wonder what the goblins have in that bucket!" Kirsty whispered.

Suddenly, the biggest goblin happened to glance around and see the baby turtles. He let out a shriek and peered nervously down at the tiny creatures.

"Look!" the goblin yelled, squinting through the darkness. "We're being followed by . . . I don't know *what* they are!"

The other two goblins spun around.

"What are you so scared of?" the

goblin with the bucket asked scornfully. "They're tiny, whatever they are. They can't hurt us!"

"They can if they're baby *pogwurzels*!" the third goblin said.

All three goblins let out frightened yelps this time.

"Ooh, pogwurzels!" cried the goblin with the bucket, backing away from the baby turtles. "I hate pogwurzels even more than I hate sand between my toes!"

"Shoo!" shouted the biggest goblin. He whipped his straw hat off and began flapping it at the baby turtles. The others did the same. "Go back to Pogwurzel Land!"

The baby turtles stayed where they were.

"They're going to attack us!" the goblin with the bucket shouted as the turtles came closer. "Run for your lives!"

All three goblins raced off along the beach in a panic, leaving the turtles behind them.

"After them!" Tess cried.

Tess and the girls flew after the goblins while Pearl followed behind, keeping an eye on the baby turtles.

When the goblins spotted Tess, Rachel,
and Kirsty flying overhead, they scowled
at them and ran even faster.

"Pesky fairies *and* scary pogwurzels!"
The biggest goblin groaned. "Go away!"

Kirsty noticed that the goblin holding the bucket was looking awfully worried. He gripped the bucket tightly with both hands, keeping it very close to him.

"What's in your bucket?" Kirsty called as she, Tess, and Rachel flew alongside the goblins.

"None of your business!" the goblin yelled. "I'm *not* telling you that we found—" The biggest goblin skidded to a halt and clapped his hand over the first goblin's mouth.

"Don't tell them anything!" he ordered angrily. "Those fairies are just trying to trick us into telling them that—"

Quickly the third goblin clapped *his* hand over the biggest goblin's mouth.

"Don't tell them our secret, blabbermouth!" he shouted.

Furiously, the biggest goblin slapped his hand away.

"Now the fairies and the pogwurzels *know* that we have a secret!" he snapped.

"You've said too much!"

"No, I haven't!" the third goblin retorted. "They don't know that we found the—"

"*Shhhh!*" The first and second goblins hushed him frantically. "Don't say anything!"

"I think there's a missing piece of the golden conch shell in that bucket," Kirsty whispered to Rachel and Tess.

"I'm going to take a look!"

As the goblins argued about what
they should or shouldn't say, Kirsty flew
toward the goblin with the bucket. Just
as she was about to peek inside it, the
goblin spotted her.

"Leave me alone!" he shouted,
whipping the bucket away from Kirsty.

"Let's help Kirsty by distracting the
goblins," Tess murmured to Rachel, and
they flew to join her.

"Be careful," Rachel called. "The baby pogwurzels are catching up with you!"

All three goblins moaned in terror as Tess and Rachel fluttered around them.

"The pogwurzels are going to nibble our toes!" the goblin with the bucket yelped.

As he turned to glance at the baby turtles, who were indeed getting closer, Kirsty saw her chance. She flew down once again. This time, she managed to get a glimpse inside the bucket.

Sure enough, there lay a piece of the missing golden conch shell, glinting in the moonlight!

Pearl and a Plan

Excited, Kirsty waved wildly at Rachel and Tess.

"It's here!" she mouthed silently, pointing at the bucket.

The goblins hadn't noticed Kirsty this time. They were huddled together, staring in panic at the baby turtles. The turtles, unaware of the goblins' fright, were patiently waiting for them to start moving again.

"We can't get away from these baby pogwurzels," the biggest goblin muttered. "They're going to follow us all the way back to Jack Frost's Ice Castle!"

"Then Jack Frost will be *really* angry with us," the third goblin added. "We need a plan to get away from them. Any ideas?"

"We could jump in the ocean and swim away," the goblin with the bucket suggested.

"That's a great idea," said the biggest goblin eagerly.

"Except that we can't swim!" the third goblin snapped.

As the goblins squabbled, Kirsty flew

quickly over to Rachel and Tess.

"We need a plan, too!" Kirsty whispered. "How are we going to get the shell piece out of that bucket?"

"We also need to stop the baby turtles from following the goblins, and lead them back to the ocean," Rachel added.

Tess's face lit up. "Pearl can help us do *both*!" she replied with a beaming smile. "Come on, girls!"

The three friends left the goblins to their arguing and flew along the beach back to where Pearl was waiting for them. Tess dipped down and whispered something to her. Pearl agreed, nodding her head.

"What do you think their plan is?" Rachel whispered to Kirsty. Kirsty could only shrug.

Rachel and Kirsty watched as Pearl began to move toward the baby turtles, pulling herself along the sand with her flippers. As Pearl got closer, her shell began to glow with dazzling fairy magic, as bright as the moon shining above them.

Slowly, the baby turtles turned their heads to look at the glowing light of Pearl's shell. Losing interest in the goblins, they all turned and hurried over to Pearl instead.

"Look!" shouted the biggest goblin with relief. "The baby pogwurzels are going away!"

"Yippee!" yelled the other goblins. They jumped up and down with glee.

"Let's go home to Jack Frost right now," the goblin with the bucket suggested. "He's going to be *very* happy when he sees what we've found!"

The biggest goblin nodded. "Give me the bucket," he said. "It's my turn to carry it."

"No, it isn't!" The goblin with the bucket hugged it protectively against him. "You can't have it!"

"Stop arguing, you two," said the third goblin. "*I'll* carry the bucket!" The goblins were so busy fighting

over the bucket, they didn't notice that
Pearl was now leading the crowd of
baby turtles right at them!

Rachel, Kirsty, and Tess watched as
the baby turtles followed Pearl closer
to the goblins. In just a few
moments, the goblins were
completely surrounded by
lots of scampering turtles.
Suddenly, the biggest
goblin looked down
and shrieked.
"The pogwurzels
snuck up
on us!" he
cried. "We're
trapped!"
"Help!" shouted
the goblin with the

bucket. In a panic, he let go of the handle.

As the bucket hit the sand, the glittering piece of the golden conch shell fell out and rolled toward Tess and the girls. Instantly, Rachel swooped down and picked it up.

"Those fairies have our shell!" the biggest goblin yelled. "We have to get it back!"

"We can't," cried the goblin who had dropped the bucket. "We're surrounded by baby pogwurzels!"

"Just a minute . . ." The third goblin frowned as he peered more closely at the baby turtles around them. The glow from Pearl's shell was lighting up the darkness and making the turtles more visible. "I don't think these are baby pogwurzels," the goblin announced at last. "They don't look scary at all. It's just another fairy trick!"

The goblins scowled at Rachel, Kirsty, and Tess.

"Give us our shell piece back!" the biggest goblin demanded.

Tess turned to Rachel and Kirsty.

"We have to take the shell back to Fairyland before the goblins can grab it," Tess said urgently. "But first we need to guide the baby turtles safely to the ocean!"

Four Found, Three to Go!

Tess beckoned to Pearl, who nodded. The turtle hurried in the direction of the ocean, her shell still glowing brightly. The baby turtles began to follow her.

Tess waved her wand around herself, Rachel, and Kirsty as they hovered in the air. A shimmering, silvery light surrounded them.

"Now the baby turtles will follow us, as well as Pearl," Tess told the girls.

Bathed in the shining glow, Tess, Rachel, and Kirsty flew toward the ocean.

"The turtles are coming!" Kirsty called with delight as she looked down and saw all the babies rushing to the water.

"STOP!" the biggest goblin roared, chasing after Tess and the girls. "Give us back the shell!"

"*She* has it!" the third goblin yelled, pointing at Rachel as she flew past him. "Grab her!"

"We can't reach her," the biggest goblin said with dismay. "There are too many of *these*!"

He pointed down at the crowds of baby turtles at his feet. There were so many of them, they were creating a barrier between Rachel and the goblins. Rachel sighed with relief, clutching the shell piece more firmly.

The turtles were now slipping into the water and swimming safely away as

Pearl, Tess, Rachel, and Kirsty watched over them. As the last turtles scurried up to the water's edge, the goblins glanced at each other.

"We can get the shell piece now!" the biggest goblin shouted triumphantly. "Come on!"

"We need to get back to Fairyland right now!" Tess cried.

With a burst of golden sparkles from Tess's wand, Pearl shrank down to fairy-size.

Then the four of them were whisked
away on a cloud of fairy magic, leaving
the goblins standing on the beach,
jumping up and down with rage.

A few seconds later, Tess, Rachel,
and Kirsty were back at the Royal
Aquarium. Shannon, Ally, Amelie, and
Pia were waiting for them, all looking
very excited. Pearl was already back
in her tank, next to Echo the dolphin,
Silky the seal, and Scamp the penguin.

The other magic ocean creatures were thrilled to see that Pearl was back! They splashed around in their tanks, waving their hellos.

"That was close," Tess said with a smile. "But we just made it!"

"Good job, everyone!" Shannon beamed at them. "Now let's replace another missing piece of the golden conch shell!"

Rachel handed her the fragment of shell.

Shannon walked over to the table where
the pieces that had already been found
were sitting on a golden stand. As
Shannon held the shell out in front of
her, there was a flash of dazzling light
and the fragment
sprang from Shannon's
hand. It fused
magically with the
other pieces, leaving no
crack.

"Only three more pieces
to find before our golden
conch shell will be whole again!"
Shannon said happily. She turned to
Rachel and Kirsty. "It's getting dark in
Leamouth, so it's time to send you home,
girls. Thank you again."

"Thank you," the fairies chorused as a

shower of magic sparkles from Shannon's wand floated down around Rachel and Kirsty. "See you again soon!"

The girls waved good-bye. A few seconds later, they found themselves back on the beach in Leamouth near their sandcastle.

"Wasn't that an exciting fairy adventure, Rachel?" Kirsty sighed happily. Then she gave a gasp. "Look at our sandcastle!"

A beautiful silver flag, glittering in the last rays of the sun, had been placed on top of one of the towers.

"Fairy magic!" Rachel exclaimed. "I'm so glad we found another shell piece, Kirsty. And we helped all the baby sea turtles get safely into the ocean, too."

"Yes—and now it's time for us to go home!" Kirsty laughed as they ran off toward her gran's cottage. "The magic did come to us, didn't it, Rachel? Even though we had to wait until the very end of the day!"

Rachel nodded. "I hope we find another piece of the magic conch shell tomorrow," she added. "Four found, three to go!"

THE OCEAN FAIRIES

Tess the Sea Turtle Fairy has found
her piece of the golden conch shell!
Now Rachel and Kirsty must help

Stephanie
the Starfish Fairy!

Join their next underwater adventure
in this special sneak peek. . . .

Starry Skies

"The ocean sounds so much louder at night, doesn't it?" Kirsty Tate said to her best friend, Rachel Walker. They were making their way down to Leamouth beach in darkness. Stars twinkled in the sky above them and a full moon cast silvery streaks on the waves.

"It feels completely different at night,"

Rachel agreed. "No noisy sea gulls, no ice-cream trucks, no families making sandcastles . . ."

Kirsty smiled. "It's really nice," she said, hugging herself to keep warm as a cool breeze swept in from the water. "Just like everything else about this vacation!"

Tonight they'd been invited to join Gran's astronomy club for an evening picnic on the beach.

Kirsty and Rachel helped set the food out as the guests arrived. Then, as the sky grew darker still, Gran pointed out some of the constellations.

An excited cheer went up among the astronomy club members at that moment, and the girls saw that some of them were pointing at the sky. "A shooting star!" Gran exclaimed. "Well, I never. That's very special. Make a wish, girls!"

"I wish we could meet another Ocean Fairy soon," Rachel murmured at once.

Kirsty heard her.

"That's what I wished for, too," she whispered.

Perfectly Princess

Don't miss these royal adventures!

Pink Princess Rules the School — Pretty Pink Pages Inside! — Alyssa Crowne

Purple Princess Wins the Prize — Pretty Purple Pages Inside! — Alyssa Crowne

Green Princess Saves the Day — Pretty Green Pages Inside! — Alyssa Crowne

Orange Princess Has a Ball — Pretty Orange Pages Inside! — Alyssa Crowne

Blue Princess Takes the Stage — Pretty Blue Pages Inside! — Alyssa Crowne

Yellow Princess Gets a Pet — Pretty Yellow Pages Inside! — Alyssa Crowne

Printed on colored pages!

RAINBOW magic™

There's Magic in Every Series!

The Rainbow Fairies

The Weather Fairies

The Jewel Fairies

The Pet Fairies

The Fun Day Fairies

The Petal Fairies

The Dance Fairies

The Music Fairies

The Sports Fairies

The Party Fairies

Read them all!

RAINBOW magic™
SPECIAL EDITION

Three Books in Each One— More Rainbow Magic Fun!

■SCHOLASTIC
www.scholastic.com
www.rainbowmagiconline.com